LOVE, LOSS AND **DEFEAT**

Yandy M. Gilson

Love, Loss and Defeat

ISBN: 978-0-692-03712-6

ATTENTION: SCHOOL AND BUSINESSES

This book is available at quantity discounts with bulk purchase for educational, business, or sales promotional use. For information and inquiries, please email ymmg23@gmail.com.

Printed in the United States of America

Fifty-three

The number of years you walk this earth

Teaching me all that you know

And some more

I hope I continue to make you proud

Beyond the grave

Beyond the clouds

Throughout the end of times

Until we meet again

~ **Daddy**

TABLE OF CONTENT

Introduction

Where should I start?

How do I begin?

This book is a collection of feelings throughout my existence. From experiences I am an old soul, I have been through a lot, and have released it all back to the universe in form of writing. So, I write for my release, my inner peace, and sanity. Though very private, I decided to share my experiences with you who's willing to read them. Hopefully, what I have been through can help someone, somehow. There's a light at the end of the tunnel, you just have to keep going, this I promise.

The Trauma

The trauma that comes to shape up our lives, they bring us pain and serves as guides. The life lessons we learned without our consent; the ones that come unexpectedly to bend or break. It's the abandonment, the accidents, the heartbreaks and death, the mistakes, the separations, the breakups that nearly caused our death. The aftermath of those traumas can leave behind, an emptiness, a void, a pain so unbearable inside. We all have been through one too many because they are inevitable. But our perception, reaction, and our ability to heal allows us to continue to be.

If you are going through the traumas, keep going. If there's not a blessing, there's a lesson in the end.

Mommy dearest

Where were thy, through the bumps

The bruises, and the broken dreams

Mommy dearest, you were nowhere to be found

Growing up

So many memories, created only in my imagination

Because you were absent

My soul felt defeated

I don't know if I should be

Sad

Hurt

Or angry

Your abandonment

Left so many issues

Hard to connect

Hard to love

Even my worth

Was hard to process

You let a little girl leave

Without any hope at all

The worse part for me was that

You did not come to look for me *at all*

I searched and searched until there was no more

I chased all dreams and daydream

Just to imagine the image of your face

A trace of your eyes

A glimpse of your smile

Just a glance

A glance of your *face*

When I heard the news

That you were no longer present in this existence

I cried

I don't know why

But I cried hard

For some reason, it still hurt

Maybe because now

All the hopes of *reconciliation* are gone

Grandma

I must say this out loud
You didn't birth me

Yet you raised

In a way

I didn't even know

I wasn't your own

You were the only mother

I've ever known

Thank you for stepping in

To fill in the void that tried to consume me

You were so delicate

So gentle

And your love

Carried me through most of it all

Your love was substantial

However, it couldn't save me through it all
It couldn't heal me from it all

Couldn't protect me them all

The world is a cruel place after all

You can never fully protect your children

From it all

I remember vividly

Some of my childhood memories

Like when I got stung by a bee

As I mistakenly step on it

I yelled and cried

'Mama I got burned' while holding my foot

By what my child, there's no fire here

But I insisted as I continue to cry

Mama went on a hunt for the fire

But found the bee with broken wings

Wriggling trying to fly after being stepped on

She told me it was just a bee

But I didn't care it hurt like fire

Since I didn't have anything else for comparison

She didn't berate me for not wearing my sandals

Instead, she cleans my up, wipes my feet

And calmed me down with some bread and tea

That's the type of person my gramma was

A gentle giant who loved felt even after ***her absent***

After school,

I had a routine

Walk to my grandpa house

Do my homework, eat dinner

Then my uncle would bring me home

This day, however, uncle wasn't home

Sun was going down

Grandpa was getting worried

He didn't want grandma coming to look for me

'I'll take her home,' he said

I know where her grandmother stays

I'm not sure why my grandpa *trusted him*

When I didn't

Riding on this man

They trusted him to take me home

But something doesn't feel right

Just as I thought he detoured

I told him that's not where to go
He told me this would be a minute

There's somewhere he had to be

He stopped at an abandoned house and ordered me to get off

He then pursued to sit on the balcony and pull me towards his lap

I tried to pull my hand from his, but instead, he grabbed the other

Now both my arms were in one hand, and he told me to be quiet

He will only hurt me if I start making noise, so I better not scream

He slowly put his hand up my skirt and removed my little girl panties

My heart throbbing so hard I can hear it in my eardrums

I couldn't hear anything else,

I just wanted to run

He went on to touch, play and fingered with my private parts

Tears are now rolling on an empty canvas of confusion,

It felt like a *nightmare*

A nightmare I never woke up from

They say *blood is thicker than water*

Is that so

The most pain I felt

Have been from the hands of those

Who were near

And supposed to be dear

But with them

I've experienced catastrophic pains

Some of the greatest threats

And biggest regrets

Summer full of rain and things

Summer back home with the family

Summer days are long and strained
Summer back in 98' I went

Playing it over in my head again

Trying to pinpoint where did it all begin

I always get lost at that part

When I replay it again and again

My dearest *cousin*

You're like a brother to me

I couldn't wait for the summers for us to be

Running in the yard, playing until nightfall

And beating our other cousins in basketball

So, every summer I would fly down

Without any hesitation at all

Until that summer in 98

When I was 11, do you remember

It was a hot summer day

I guess I was changing

My body started developing

Who knew

What would have transpired

When you were left alone me

Your mind was way advanced

More experienced

Maybe that is why

You look at me differently

And because of that

You stole something from me

My innocent

Was for me to keep

To give at my own free will

Yet you stole it from me

How could you do that to me

Held down in captivity

Frozen and confused

At eleven what the heck did I knew
I asked over and over

What's going on

What are you doing

Please stop I cried

Please

Please

Feels like I was fighting for my life, but I'm losing

He is too big, too strong

The pain so unbearable

I cried out loud, yelled, kicked and screamed
Hoping someone would hear

But no one's home

No one is coming to my rescue

So, as the tears rolling down my face

Entered my eardrums, and soaked the bed
I just *cried out*

And prayed for it to be over

What just happened

I'm not sure

But I felt like

Something just pierced my soul

And I will never be the same again

Never

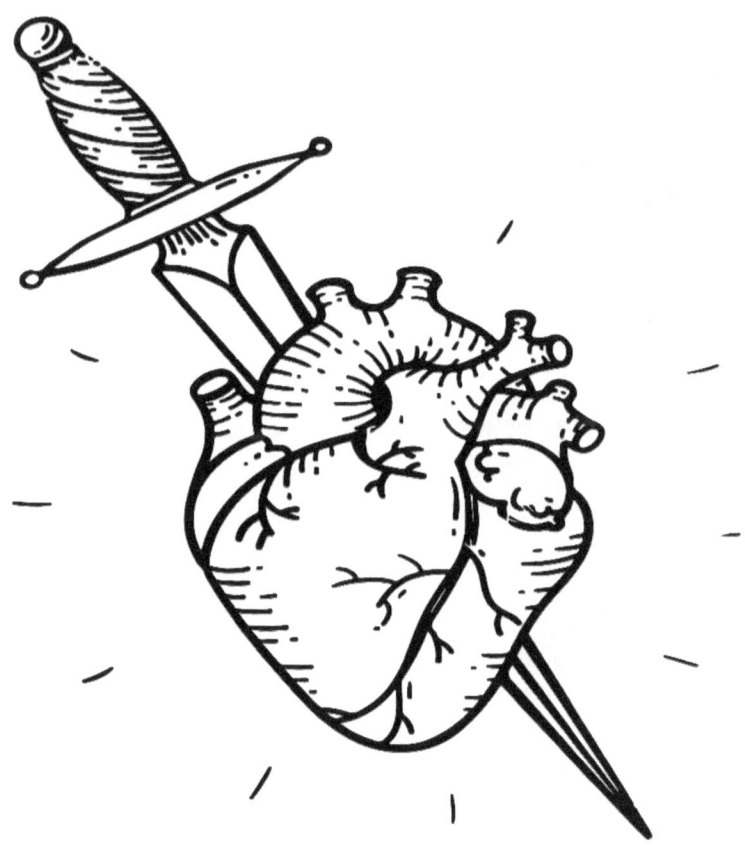

I don't care what's in our DNA

I don't care if we're old and grey

There's no religion in hell

That could make me ever forgive you

Close we will never be

I chop you off the family tree

You no longer exist to me

When you see me

Don't smile

Don't act like you forgot

Don't say hi

When folks are around

Guilt should overcome you

Whenever you see my face

Your conscious should make you *stay away*

Because this right here

Will never go away

So please,

Stay the hell away

You're all messed up

But don't have a clue

This life of yours will be full of

Broken promises

Broken dreams

Broken family

And many *broken things*

Little girl

Where you going

Growing up so fast

What makes you in a hurry

Life's coming at your fast

Slow your role

Trying to fill the void

When you're not even whole

Little girl

Slow your role

I flew back home

For my grandmothers' funeral

To pay my respect to a beautiful being

Getting her wings

But I couldn't grieve properly

Because both my *predators* were there

Mingling with the crowed

And had the audacity to attempt small talks

High school

Hormones growing

Peer pressure rising

Teenagers doing

What grown folks doing

Not even sure

Totally clueless

I fell in love

With a **boy like you**

6'2

Brown eyes

Luscious lips

Just formulating my type

Wasn't sure

If you knew

But you gave me a glance of hope

I fell deep

I fell hard

9th, 10th, 11th even 12th

You had my heart

Together or apart

Fast in love

Fast in lust

I didn't care

As long as I had his heart

I knew we had a *chance at love*

He told me I was **beautiful**

And for once I believed it

Like his validation

Was all I needed

To feel that I was worth it

I was seen

By his big brown eyes

He noticed me

In the crowed full of possibilities

He lifted my spirit

He glorified my being

He loved me

Just by me being me

Here I am *Daydreaming*

Of my happy ending

Planning my future

Nothing was more certain

Then you being in it

Because life without you

Would be like a sky with no stars

An ocean with no blues

And simply

I just couldn't live in it

A *baby*

No way, this can't be

Tell me this is all a dream

Pinch me now, because this can't be real

Not my fairytale, not my happy ending

No, just no

Tell me you are kidding

Tell me this is a joke

But the look on his face said it all
 As tears cloud my vision

All things became blurry

And you said you loved me

Let it sink in

You loved me

Well if this is love

Then I don't want it

I rather wrap it around a rock

Throw it in the ocean

And let contaminate the part

Where no life exists

My first heartbreak

Was the residue of you

Your lies

Your mischief

Your deceit

Was long over due

For me to finally say I'm through

Trust me, you have outdone your do's

So, I put the hopes of us to rest

As I lay in my bed

I couldn't help but *wept,* and wept

I'm detaching
From all things foreign
Outside of the air
I'm breathing
This pain runs too deep
It hard to process
I can't sleep
I can't eat
My heart aches
My heart breaks
I wish this numbness
Would go away
A week went by
Down ten pounds
I wonder
Are you happy now

On the verge of depression

I feel it sliding in

It's crazy the feeling a heartbreak can bring

The empty feelings of nothingness

Anticipating too crawl in

Deep within

To *swallow me whole*

And leave me lonely at most

Don't let heartbreaks

Make you cold

Always be willing

To *love once more*

Even if it hurts

Try it one more

At least that's what I was told

I have abonnement issues
So, after the heartbreak
I hated all men
I was focused on my money
And my books
In college full-time
Working two jobs
When I met you
I clearly stated my position
You decided to be down for the cause
I was very closeminded
Did not want to be bothered
Yet you knocked
And knocked
Until the *walls* started coming down

When I met him
There was something about him
That was different

A new rhythm like afro beats
He made my *soul dance*
I started two stepping
The rhythm drew me in

 Maybe it was his cologne
Maybe it was his favorite song
Whatever it was finally
I felt like maybe it's okay
Okay to smile again

College life

Out of town

Out of sight

Out of mind

As we explore

Who we wanted to be

What we ought to be

What we inspired to be

Together we were

Carving our history

Full of vivid memories

The two of us

Just worked

We left home

And created our own

While we find ourselves

In the vast of possibilities

And together we achieved some of that

FAMU class of 09

Damn, those were the best of times

Some of the best years of my life

Was spend writing down

The dreams of our happy ending

That *never came to be*

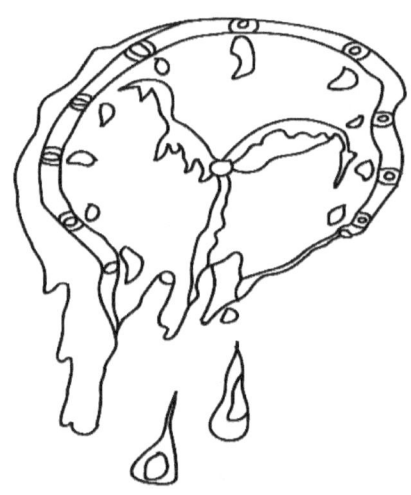

The first sign of the real world

Budgeting paycheck

Balancing checkbooks

Living off Ramen Noodles

Waiting on the next payday

Getting paid

Just to be broke again the next day

But all that didn't matter

I was happy I was in it with you"

Who would of thought

After what we been through

You weren't done

Rounding around

But you knew

Here I am again

Clueless

I was too busy

Planning out our next chapter

She was the new-new

Who became your mused

Overnight

She became your jewel

And made you forget

About our chemistry

Our dialect Our history

Three years felt like seconds

As they *disintegrated*

Through my fingers

Like water

In a drought

Like flames

Burning out

So, into the night

You disappear

With my hopes

My dreams

My heart and all

What's left of the girl

Who lost herself

In the web of lies that you told

Back and forth you went

Toyed with her emotions

What become of that girl

Who loved you to the bone

But lost it all in return

She too dreamed big

And loved hard

But now she wonders

What for She gives and gives

And gives much more

Her heart, her soul

Whatever, it was yours

But what the hell for

Pillows all wet

Hair's a mess

Nose all stuffy

Can't catch a breath

Pop a pill and lay to rest

Sleep will eventually come

Hopefully before the crack of dawn

And the *cycle goes on* and on

Something is boiling

Something unhealthy

Is unveiling

When too much pain

And too much frustration

Clashes

The outcome

Can become *dangerous*

This is anger

At its rarest form

Anger

Like you never known

I hate you

To my very core

I cursed

The day you were born

They day your daddy met your mom

I wished she would have told him no

Or at least abort your behind

When she found out you were forming

In her womb

I wished them tubes

Had wrapped around your neck

Before you came out

And took your very first breath

Anything

The worse imaginable

To spare me from this pain

Angry black woman

I was that

Looking back

I owned that

I was a wreck

At this point

I couldn't care any less

That's why when we met

I was broken

I didn't hide my scars

They were wide open

Running away from pain

Running away from shame

In search of a quick fling

To make me feel like a woman again

I wanted to be wanted

Since he was out there running

With her

I didn't give myself time to heal

Because I wasn't looking for something real

I just jump

Headfirst

From the frying pan

Into the fire

And here I was

In the fire

Dancing and Burning

Like an *avalanche*

Everything's unraveling

Too quickly

I'm spinning

Running

Clubbing

Hurting

Going to sleep angry

Waking up crying

Still reminiscing

What the hell am I doing

Here and now

With him

When I'm still hurting

Over him

Before I can pull my head up

To catch my breath

And really get a grasp

Of what's going on

My carelessness

Got me stuck

Right upon my exit

Slowly my life

Became this *rollercoaster*

I couldn't control the outcomes

I was just numb

Going through the motions

But not really living

Trying to figure what was happening

How did I end up here

I don't know

Slowly he is moving in

Everything's going so fast

Yet in slow motion

I just couldn't grasp it

Tired of all this fighting

Going out to the club partying

While I am home

Sick

He's out enjoying

His many women

Yes, there were rumors

Of many

But I tried not to stress

Not to say to a word

Tried not to care

But this night

I was fed up

So, I packed him up

While he was gone for a day or two

Without me having a clue

When he finally came home

His eviction noticed was at the door

Along with all the little things he owned

He was not happy

So furious, his eyes lit up like fire

And from there *it begins*

The *first time* it happened

Was when the eviction noticed was at the door

Eyes lit up like flames, filled with anger and hate He
raised his hand and stretch it wide

When the palm of his hands connected

They did so on my left cheek

The force knocked me to my knees

Holding on to him

So, I wouldn't fall flat on my face

He raised his hand again

And he struck

I started crying

Blood started gushing in my mouth

Stop!

I cried Please!

As I laid down at his feet

Surrendering
Protecting my 8 months belly

My baby started to kick

Outside looking in

There are so many things

I could have done

At that point to change the *outcome*

But while leaving in this nightmare

All I thought about was my child

And the fact that he would grow up without a father

For that fear alone, I silenced my cries

As I tried to figure all this out

Born into this chaos

Was hope

Dressed up like a little prince

In his eyes

I found love

What I've been longing for

All along

He ignited my spirit

Set fire to my fears

And gave me a reason to live

So perfectly unplanned

There was he

As beautiful as he possibly can

Now I try to live for him

I'm in and out of consciousness

It all starts to sink in

I really started wondering

Could this be it how it all ends

I'm trying to stop him

But his hands are so tightly wrapped

Around my neck

I can't get a grip

Can't catch a breath

All he sees is red

I'm fighting to *catch a breath*

Everything is getting dark

He is too big

Too powerful

Too strong

And simply

I can't hold on much longer

I wanted to be happy

With the joy this little boy brought

I didn't prioritize my relationship

I stayed in my lane to stay under his radar

But he would randomly catch these fits

And something would quickly take over

A second, he is good

A second later I'm fighting for my very ***existence***

A fear so profound he bought

Every time I let him get near

He pried on my weakness

Took advantage of my brokenness

Used my past against me

And told me I was worthless

He *isolated* me from it all

Family

Friends

Self

Something has to give

Something has to change

Or I won't make it to the end

Love tarnished

The vivid image of what it was supposed to be

But you're left with the ugly reality

Of what it never was

Emotionally abused

Seeking love from the wrong dudes

Self-love is something unheard of

Clearly, you're not good enough

For anyone to love you

Or for even loving yourself

At least that is what he made you believed

Questioned

Everything that once made you...you

Unsure of the image that stares back at you

When you look in the mirror

Surely there's something in there

You can identify with

You're bruised and battered

Emotionally

Physically

Spiritually

Drained

Yet you're still wishing

That one day

He will change

I have abandonment issues

I don't want him to have them too

For that reason, I convinced myself to

To stay

When my departure was long overdue

I stayed

I took all the blows

The slaps

The punches

And the busted lips

Make-up was my cover-up

Overnight I became a Covergirl

Lied to my co-workers

Stayed away from friends

They may ask question

I can't begin to explain

Stayed away from family too

As I continued to

Make excuses for him

He will do better

He will get better

But he never did

Never

At night

These wicked thoughts start seeping in

Going at it once again

When will it stop

Will it ever end

Eyes closed

But my mind is at war

War from within

So many voices going in

Fighting my worst enemies again

All the problem's rolling in

It's been pouring for so long

When will this ever end

I feel boxed in

Suffocating

No air coming in

I've been here so long

In this picture,

In this frame

In this space,

In this thing

Maybe I've gotten so used to the pain

That I don't know who I'll be once it ends

As I was going through the cycles

You were going through *your trials*

Your health deuterating

What a horrible disease

This diabetes

I tried my best to be there for you

While I was going through it

The many days I kept from you

Was when I couldn't bear for you to see it

I know you had too much on plate

To worry about your daughter's swollen face

In your presence I couldn't lie

So, I rather hide

And tell that I'm alright

Dad,

Trust me

I'm alright

I remember the day I took you to the hospital
I brought my son over to bring you a little joy
Hoping he would be an encouragement
To bring you back *home*

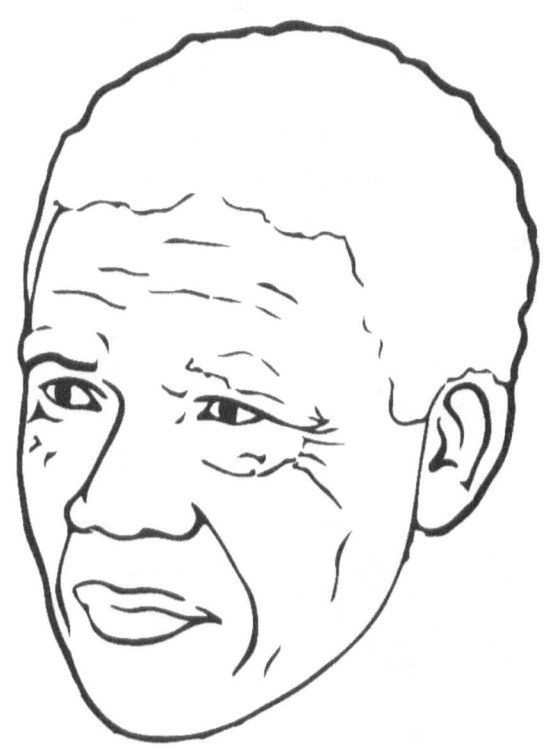

There came a time when I stopped praying for myself

 For my situation was hopeless

The only time I went on my knees

Was for my father

I would go on my knees

Bargaining with God

Of all the things I would do differently

If He allows him to come home

Days turned into weeks

Weeks into months

You fell into a coma

And you never came back home

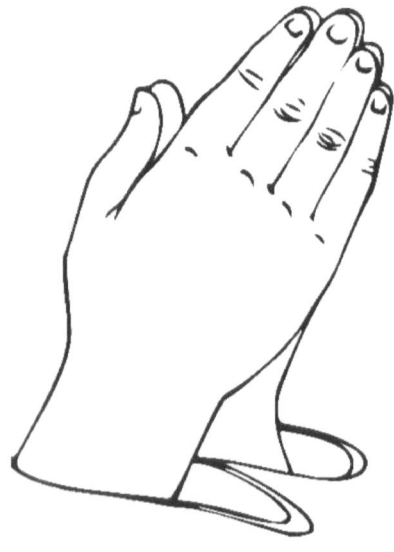

When I got the call

Sorry we tried it all

I started screaming,

No! Please! Please! No!

I felt like my soul left my body

And started floating above me

Because the pain was too immense

For it to survive in there

On the 8th of March

The year twenty twelve

You took your last glance

Your last breath

As you say goodbye to this world

You said *goodbye* to your one and only child

I cried a ***river of tears***

Feels like my tears dried up

Life has left me

To empty

To cry

To feel

To need

Anything physiological

If it wasn't for my son

I would return

To the dust I once was

People grief differently
I found comfort in the *little things*
Like replaying your voicemails
Over and over again
To simply hear your voice
I even used to text your number
Long after it was disconnected
To tell you about my day
To carry on the conversations
Like you never left

My mentor

My idol

My motivator

My friend

The one who held my hands

Help me to stand

On my own two feet

Simply with the words he speaks

I remember driving down Parkland

Where the big houses stand

Telling me one day

One will be mine

I smiled

Not because I believed him

But because I was proud

That he thought of me this way

Yet he could not stay

To see the day

When I buy that mansion on the hills

His purpose was fulfilled

After he handed me my dreams

For this reason

I will continue

To **make him proud**

Long after he is gone

Every time I took a step forward

I took five steps back

I was running out of energy

There were no future plans

No commitment

No change

Just living in the presence

Trying to live to the fullest

When I'm merely only ***existing***

Baby boy started growing

He started noticing

That mommy wasn't happy

And sometimes that made him unhappy

That's the courage I needed

To finally walk away

From something so unhealthy

That's been happening for years

Six years was more than enough

For this man to shape up

Lord knows I tried

To make this family dynamic work

But he still running these streets

I decided to set him free

And set *fire to that bridge*

As you can see

I fought many battles

Like a soldier I went to war

But in the end, I came up short

I lost many *battles*

Lost the mother that I never knew

Lost my darling grandmother

Lost my beloved father

Lost many more

To physical and emotional abused

I guess when the time is right

I will start winning some

And hopefully no longer have to fight

So now you see what I mean

When I tell you I've been broken

Physically and mentally

Drained from all emotions

I've tried them all

I've seen them all

And now

I rebuke them all

Cleansing from it all

I'm fasting

The trauma they do linger

Like a wound that fester

And refuse to heal

But I'm fasting

Until I'm properly heal

From it all

I'm *fasting*

Thankful

Through the traumas, I remained thankful. Each day I woke up, I was hopeful. Amid my depression, I was holding unto a glimpse of the future that looked a little brighter. So, I kept that thought, and although life was rough, I knew there was better out there for me. I started envisioning a future away from the chaos, a peaceful place where joy feels like the air the wraps around my body. There will be no space for nothing else to exist but happiness. A place where the lessons learned will be a place of gratitude to help others out of similar situations. I am at that place now, and I am thankful to be there.

Beautiful girl, where does your pain hide?

For you carrying on the world

With no discomfort on your shoulders

And always seems to crack a smile

The world never sees the ugly side of you

Because there is none

Just that pretty face painted like an oil canvas

Independent woman

Tell me where you get those strides

To work two jobs day in and day out

Working your finger to the bone

To provide for your little one

You walk around gracefully

As if you have everything that you wish

Your presence is inspiring

Your spirit gives us motivation

Girls and *women*

Both young and old

That carries it all in our soul

Give our hearts to the world

Our all to our families

The world may not recognize you

But we see you

And applaud you

Thank you

My worth I had to find
Because the world was so unkind
I thought I wasn't worth much
I thought my value couldn't be
Something that worth any sacrifice
For years, I just let it be
Let men abused me
Emotionally and physically
Because my worth wasn't worth much
In my mind, at least
It took some time
Years to be exact
To realize
I'm worth more
It took me a while
To realize how precious, I was
A piece of jewel
A rare stone
A ***black diamond***
Don't doesn't crack under pressure
So now I shine
Blissfully I shine

Dear Future Husband

I need you to love me

From the tips of my natural coil hair

To the bottom of my weary feet

Cherish each moment you spend with me

When I am no longer in your presence

I want you to long for me

I want to love the way you look at me

When you look into my eyes

I want you to see all I am trying to hide

I want you to know me, inside and out

I want you to believe

Believe in my abilities, my goals

My dreams and aspirations

Gives me the hopes I need

In humankind

I know you are going to be loving and kind

Your spirit will speak to my soul

Your courage, Lord behold

Will be stronger than I've ever known

Your love will speak louder than any words

Together we will be a force

Strengthen by God's very own hand,

So, let no man interfere

I was created for your amusement

Your pleasure, your happiness

I am your lost rib and your purpose

Of why you were chosen to be man

You will be my king

My protector, my provider

More importantly

My husband

Acknowledgement

To my little miracle boy Preston who kept me going when all hopes were lost, thank you. You're not old enough to understand the impact your life made in mine. You gave me hope to carry one, and the will to keep trying. You are the reason for my being. If I'm anything in life, it's because of you and the dreams of my father.

To my wonderful husband, I'm so glad I fasted, because of the time I took for myself, allowed me to meet and fell for the person that made for me. You accepted me with flaws and all and made believed there was purpose in my pain. I spoke, wish, dreamed you into existence. I could not pray for anything more than the love you have shown me. I continue to explore the exciting journey life has in store for us. I love you, Bruce!

To my family and friends who became family, thank you for your unwavering love, you continue to support me and believe in me in all that I do. Although my father is no longer alive, I feel his vibration and spirit in the love you guys have shown. Thank you for standing steadfast in my corner. You are all appreciated beyond words, and I'm grateful to have you all in my life.

www.ingramcontent.com/pod-product-compliance
Lightning Source LLC
Chambersburg PA
CBHW030609130626
46552CB00006B/2701